Alice in Wonderland

Fairy Tale Classics

retold by Dandi

lice sat on the river bank and watched her sister read. "What good is a book without pictures?" she complained. Then Alice noticed a quite remarkable White Rabbit. The Rabbit took a watch from his pocket and exclaimed, "Oh my ears and whiskers! I'm late!"

Alice ran after the curious Rabbit. He popped down a large rabbit hole, and Alice jumped down after him. Down, down, down she fell — on and on, past cupboards and bookshelves, and bottles and jars! Thump! Thump! Thump! She plopped down in front of a tiny, wooden door.

However shall I get in?" asked Alice.

On a tiny table sat a tiny bottle with the words 'Drink Me' written on the label. Alice did as she was told.

"Why, it tastes like cherries and turkey and toast!" she declared. "But what a curious feeling..." And with a jerk – and another – Alice shrank to the size of a foot!

t least now I can fit through that door," said Alice, walking through. "Curiouser and curiouser."

"Oh my ears and whiskers!" sang a familiar voice. "I'm late!"

"It's the White Rabbit! Wait for me!" Alice cried. And she ran to catch up with him.

$\mathcal{A}$lice followed him to a large table set out under a tree. The White Rabbit was having tea with the Mad Hatter and a snoring Dormouse!

"There's no room for you!" cried the Rabbit and the Mad Hatter.

But Alice could see there was room for a dozen of her. "There's plenty of room!" she said, taking a seat.

hat an unforgettable Tea Party! The Mad Hatter and the White Rabbit told riddles which made no sense to Alice. Then the Mad Hatter spilled his teacup and demanded Alice's clean cup. Poor Alice never did get her tea.

"This is too much!" said Alice. And she left.

lice ran through a Wonderland Woods, where she met a large, blue Caterpillar. He gave her a magic mushroom.

"One side will make you grow taller," he explained. "The other will make you smaller."

Roaming still farther, Alice met the Cheshire Cat on a bough of a tree. "Would you tell me which way to walk?" she asked.

But the cat just grinned, then disappeared.

At last Alice wandered into the most curious land yet — a world of cards! The Queen of Hearts was arguing with two of her card-soldiers. "You interrupted my croquet game!" she screamed. "Off with your heads!"

"Nonsense," said Alice. "You'll do no such thing." Then she took a bite from the 'Grow Bigger' side of the mushroom.

hy your croquet mallet is no more than a flamingo!" said Alice, bursting into laughter!

"Off with *your* head!" shouted the angry Queen of Hearts.

"Stuff and nonsense!" Alice said. For she was feeling rather brave now, having grown to her full size. "You are nothing but a pack of cards!"

At this, the whole deck came flying down on Alice! She screamed and tried to run away.

hrashing, Alice found herself on the bank again.

"Wake up, Alice!" said her sister.

"Such a curious dream," Alice said.

"It's getting late, Alice," said her sister. "Run along for tea."

Alice dashed to the house, singing to herself, "Oh, my ears and whiskers! I'm late! I'm late!"